# The Magical Land

Kiana Rostamiani

iUniverse LLC
Bloomington

# THE MAGICAL LAND

iUniverse books may be ordered through booksellers or by contacting:

iUniverse LLC
1663 Liberty Drive
Bloomington, IN 47403
www.iuniverse.com
1-800-Authors (1-800-288-4677)

ISBN: 978-1-4917-2104-9 (sc)
ISBN: 978-1-4917-2105-6 (e)

Library of Congress Control Number: 2014900773

Printed in the United States of America.

iUniverse rev. date: 01/22/2014

To my lovely, sweet sister:
Nicky

# Contents

Prologue.................................................................................ix

Chapter 1    The Truth ...........................................................1

Chapter 2    The Walk.............................................................6

Chapter 3    The Magical Land................................................. 10

Chapter 4    The Darkness....................................................... 15

Chapter 5    The Village........................................................... 19

Chapter 6    The Friendship.....................................................25

Chapter 7    The Plot ..............................................................40

Chapter 8    The Secret ...........................................................51

Chapter 9    The Return ..........................................................56

Chapter 10    Home .................................................................63

# Prologue

## I

Scared. I am very scared. I am not even supposed to be writing this now. If Grandpa finds out, he will be very angry for sure. Well, I am very tired of this life anyway. Please do not be mistaken; I like life very much. The only problem is that things get out of hand sometimes and this makes me feel frustrated. But then I remember what my mother always used to tell me: "Be strong, Amy, no matter what." This is very hard to do, though. I, personally, have not met anyone who can be strong all the time. We all need a break from the hardships of life. But I think it is important to choose the kind of break wisely and consider the consequences. After all, breaks only last for a very short time, and if it has not been chosen wisely, it will cause regret for the rest of one's life. For example, I did not enjoy my summer break when I was younger, and I am now regretting every single lost second of it, but unfortunately time has no return or exchange policy.

Oh, no. I'm hearing footsteps. It must be Grandpa.

# II

He is gone again. He left for work this morning and will not return until tonight, which is relieving to me because I can write freely while he is gone, but I also have to finish the assigned portion of my daily work. He always forces me to do my academic work on a very tight schedule and leaves no room for anything, except for studying or mental exercises. Unbelievable, you may think. It is true, I have gained some weight as well, but Grandpa ignores it. He tries to avoid the truth because he feels guilty about it. Also, my daily schedule is hilarious. After breakfast, the day starts with a tough game of chess with Grandpa, followed by a detailed study of science, including biology, chemistry, physics, and geology. Finally, the rest of the day will be spent by studying mathematical concepts, such as algebra, geometry, and calculus, and of course, all of these courses are studied at an advanced level. Sometimes when I am lucky enough and Grandpa is in a good mood, he allows me to work in the science lab, yet all I am allowed to do there is to repeat the old scientific experiments that I have already done before. He never allows me to try anything new: "No improvising, young lady," he always says. Studying all these endless courses makes me tired at times, but I have learned to be submissive about it because whenever I ask him if there is anything else that I could do, he always places another pile of work in front of me, and says with a wide grin, "Of course! Dig in!" And when I get bored and start complaining, he becomes very angry at me. I never know why he is angry all the time, for I have never left this house much farther than the garden. I have always been listening to him and obeying every single request of his, so I cannot understand his anger and sorrow.

I tend to get tired of him sometimes, but then I remind myself that I have no one else except him and that maybe it is time to get used to him and accept him the way he is. What bothers me more than anything else is that he expects me to do all of the hard work, and all he does is switch his seat from behind the computer screen to the television set when he is at home. When he is in the right mood, he cooks dinner, but usually all our food is bought from the fast food stores. You may wonder how I am still alive when I eat these types of food everyday and do not exercise at all. The truth is that I try to exercise, as often as I can, even if that means for two or three minutes a day. Also, whenever he is not looking, I slip out of the house and into the garden to pick some fresh, lovely strawberries and blueberries since these two are the only fruits growing in our humble, small garden. I have seen him gathering the berries, washing them, and sometimes even drying them, but he's never offered one to me. As a young child, I used to stare at the berries outside and wish that I could taste one, but whenever I asked him if I could have any, he snapped at me angrily and said: "Don't you know nothing? These berries are poisonous. You wanna get sick or die?" Only later did I understand that he had been selling the berries to have a source of income. Who knows what other secrets he has been keeping from me all these years!

Sometimes I feel so trapped that I start to cry and when he is not home, I even shout for help, but it is useless because we are in a completely stranded place where no one else lives. He specifically chose this place to raise me. I am not being ungrateful. It is a beautiful place. All around us are trees of different kinds.

In front of my room is an oak tree, and how it always stays green truly fascinates me. I know the mechanism and the science behind it, but I feel that there is more to it, rather than just science. It is strange too. Whenever I look at that tree, my father comes into my mind, and when I question why things are this way, I remember him saying: "Everything has a reason, my sweet angel. You will just have to find out for yourself." True, but sometimes one cannot find the reason to many things, so to me, not everything has a reason and some things just happen by chance.

There are times when I miss my parents very much. I wish there was a way I could turn back time and bring them back to life so that only the three of us could live together. I have gotten used to knowing the truth, though. It has been such a long time since I last saw my parents, but to me it seems that only a day has passed. It feels just like yesterday that we were getting ready to go to the fair on a lovely summer evening. It was my very first time of going to the fair, and I was only seven years old. Still, it is unbelievable what a seven-years-old can do when he or she gets excited. I remember jumping and singing all day long in my excitement. My mother could hardly dress me! And when we were in the car, I was deliberately out of control. Even though my seat belt was tight, I could still make the car move by constantly jumping in my seat and singing. My father asked me to stop many times as he was driving and I was making him lose his concentration. He warned me, but I did not listen. I was so over-excited that I started to choke as a result of all my laughter. This was when my father turned around to see if I were alright, since he was a nurse and could help in the emergencies at least. My mother was trying to find a water bottle for me in her bag, when the next thing I heard was a scream. I do not remember from whom. Probably from my mother, but this does not matter because it was already too late. They both passed away in the car accident, and I unfortunately, survived. I remember the nurse telling me how great it was that I survived and what a wonderful life I was going to have, making my parents proud. But her words were like a sharp knife cutting through my broken heart. I killed them. It was all my fault. If I were quiet, like a good, obedient child, none of this would have ever happened. Or maybe if I had never been born, my parents could have had another, better child and would still be alive. It has been nine years since the accident, but I still cannot forget.

My only relation that I could live with was my Grandpa who resided in Kentucky, the same state as we used to. Except for my grandpa, I had my uncle who lived in California and did not want me around. When they were discussing my situation, my uncle kept saying, "Oh, please! I don't need another dependent. I just gave one off to my bride!" He, at that point, started laughing heartily, thinking that he had just said the funniest joke in the universe. Of course, he did not expect me to be standing behind the door, listening to his conversation, but I cannot help but listen to what people say behind my back. I think since it concerns me, I should be the first to know.

Oh, no. I hear the car . . . Later, I hope.

# III

Well, that went well. Grandpa figured out what I had been doing! He saw what I have been up to, sneaking to the computer room whenever he was not home. Apparently, he had been watching me all along, which I appreciate, but at the same time dislike. His reaction was not as I had expected, though. He came to my room and sat down on the chair in front of my crowded, little desk, and started lecturing me for exactly two hours on the disadvantages of writing! According to him, writing brings only two things with itself: Waste of precious time and trouble for others. I do not see how writing my story would hurt or cause trouble for others, but I had to agree with his points at the time since he was very upset. During this time, I could not help but stare at his long, straight, white beard and imagine how funny it would look if it were to be braided and dyed! My grandpa is also somewhat completely bald, with only traces of short, white hair around his round, shining head. As one could imagine, he is also overweight, but tries to hide his grown belly by wearing loose pajamas all day long!

"Amy? Did you understand anything I told you?" asked Grandpa.

"Huh?—Oh, yes!" responded Amy cluelessly.

"Really? Well, can you repeat what I had just told you?" asked Grandpa suspiciously.

I just cannot stand it when Grandpa asks this question! Of course I was not listening to him, but he does not need to bring it up to me this directly! Luckily, I was saved by the telephone ring, but soon grandpa retuned and continued lecturing me on how terrible it is to disobey my only caretaker and how important he should be to me, and that I should always do my best to keep him pleased after all he has done for me. Then, he insisted on reading all that I had written! This was completely impossible for me to do due to the obvious reasons! Therefore, I was forced to lie. I hate lying, but sometimes it is the only way a person can rescue him or herself from a swamp one has created earlier and avoid being pulled into the swamp any further and suffocate. I told him that I had forgotten to save my writing on the flash drive and now everything was gone. Luckily, he believed my "white lie" and seemed to be very pleased as well. Finally, he decided to leave and go to the town nearby for the "usual grocery shopping." I knew that Grandpa left the house everyday, but he always told me that he needed to go to the bank to collect some money given to us from the government. Since my grandpa is an old, retired man who was indeed a war hero, we receive some help from the government to live. Aside from the money obtained from selling the berries, the aid given to Grandpa helps us live. But he has never told me anything about his salary or about what else he does when he leaves the house, and I was never concerned enough to ask.

He is gone now, and I am alone again. Fortunately, I can still write this without his interference. The computer room is quite different than anywhere else in the house. First of all, it looks much older and darker than the other rooms but it feels much more exciting! I do not know how to express this, but I feel very happy when I come in this room. True, I may feel uncomfortable lying to my grandpa, but I am writing this with all my might in hopes of finding an ultimate peace in life, something I have searched for so long. I understand that the journey is long, but I hope I can start from somewhere. It is no use to sit in my room day after day, staring at my books helplessly, wishing something would happen and change my life. I am now sixteen years old, but I feel no different than when I was only seven. There is something wrong, only the more I spend time thinking about it, the less I understand my problem.

This computer room is not in any better condition than I am. The floor is covered with dust and dirt. Who knows the last time this place has been cleaned? I have a tendency to clean my personal work area before I start studying. If my room is not organized, I can easily lose my concentration. My Obsessive-compulsive cleaning disorder has driven Grandpa crazy over the years, but he has learned to get used to it. I would very much love to clean this room too, but I am afraid that Grandpa would notice and become angry again because no matter how much he has gotten used to allowing me to have an organized and highly cleaned area, he would still not appreciate it if I were sneaking into the computer room, as this is the place he also keeps his war records and "important treasures". Of course, with all the dust, I have been unable to see anything special here, except the gray looking computer on the small, brown table in the corner of the room. Even the computer has been tired of sitting here day after day, wishing for a change, wishing for a ray of sunlight. I know, because I can hear it moaning with the loud sounds it makes whenever it is turned on or off, but I know what is wrong with this room, and even with this house: it is lonely.

In fact, there have been many times when even I have felt like the loneliest person in the whole world, but then I remind myself that maybe I am the luckiest as well! I do not believe that many people would have the opportunity to live with a war hero and study all the time, in hopes of becoming an important individual in the future. However, I would give up all of this just to spend a day outside by myself. Nobody knows what great adventures I would have then. Once, my grandpa notified me about the danger of the outside world. He told me that the only real adventure I was going to have outside was being eaten by wild animals. I have not been able to believe him, though. I think I am being eaten inside this "Safe" house much faster. Also, it is not like I have never been in the society! Before my parents passed away, I used to go outside with them quite often, and I know that the outside world is to be admired and enjoyed, even though Grandpa has been telling me that it has all changed. He may be doing this to keep me safe, but I do not understand the necessity of this since we are located in an almost completely stranded area.

# IV

So, Grandpa came back with a new book for me today, called the "Advanced Economy". I am told that it is from the local library, but it looks very old and difficult. Even though I am used to studying, sometimes using very old books, I have never seen any books as old as this! One of Grandpa's famous expressions is that "Good books are the old books". I do not know if this belief is due to his personal problems with the current, revised, and modern educational system, or due to the exceptionally high costs of new books. All I know is that he always wants me to read and study using the books published during the late of 20th century. Now, this book is dated back in the beginning 20th century! It is unbelievably old! My Grandpa has already, somehow either bought this ancient book or has found it somewhere because I can see no markings or signs from the library. But when I asked him how he had gotten hold of the book, he only responded, "From the local library, but I am certain that you will enjoy this much more than your 'little writing' habit, so just finish the book, and as usual, write its report at the end."

Grandpa always makes me write a report at the end of each book that I finish. According to Grandpa, the report should contain all the information presented in the book in a detailed, but concise manner, and easy enough that someone without a prior knowledge would understand. After I turn in the report, he usually pulls out some questions and gives them to me to "examine my learning". My responses must have sounded very well to him, so he rarely bothers me with hard questions often. But now that I am looking at this thick, old, dusty book, I feel frustrated and scared. I have never thought about failure before. What if I cannot do this?

# V

Today was the first day of summer, and I spent my entire day dealing with the ancient book. Not only does it smell like an old, damp book, but it is extremely difficult to understand and analyze as well, and I have no help whatsoever. While it is true that I have never had any considerable amount of help from Grandpa or anyone else before, I have never received such difficult information either. Grandpa also has a rule of assigning a "due date" for each book that I receive, and on the due date, he will ask for the report and will quiz me as well. I only remember one time when I was unable to answer one of the questions on a book. It was on my first mathematics book, and when I failed, he made me copy the whole book completely. I will never forget that, and this is why I am scared. I never failed again and cannot imagine what would happen if I do. I have studied and learned so much that if I were to write a book about my knowledge, it may become one of the thickest and most amazing books ever written, but I am not willing to do that at all. I need to place some distance from studying and focus on myself more.

I miss my parents all the time and wish that there was a way I could bring them back to life. But then I ask myself, "why should I?" "What is the purpose of life?" "Why are humans created, and why do they die?" I have learned that "Why" may not be a very logical question to ask. If I were to rephrase my questions, I would ask: "How do humans die and exactly how are their souls created?" I have been in search for answers to these fundamental questions for years, but I have found no logical proof or response. Maybe I am not searching hard enough or maybe I need to find a different path. For example, some believe in the existence of a "Super-human intelligence" that is governing the world, but we, as humans, do not know much about this great power. Even though it is extremely difficult to answer these questions, I need to come up with some answers in order to feel like a mature human being. I feel that there is a huge empty space inside of my soul without these answers, and I cannot wait until I discover some.

The truth is that I have been designing an instrument or a machine. This machine will give human beings an amazing power. They will become invincible with it, and mortal without it. I call this instrument a Reverse machine. Now, I am not certain about its function yet, since I have not tested it, but I hope to find out soon. I have been doing extensive amount of work on this and I only wish that my ideas would make logical sense. I have been working on this ever since moving in with Grandpa. I thought about it, came up with new ideas, and even sketched them. Of course, I did all of this while Grandpa was not noticing, for he would have been completely outraged if he found out. The only reason for me to have come up with this idea was a childish dream of bringing my parents back to life, which I highly doubt may happen. Since I was very young when I lost them, and I lost them in such a traumatic way, I could not truly believe that they were gone. Grandpa has not been very helpful either. He thought that by confining me to this small cottage, he would make sure of my safety; he thought by giving me an extreme amount of work, he would make certain of my health and would educate me well. I sometimes wonder: Educate me for what reason? I have read that people become educated in order to work and serve in the society. I know I will never be allowed to leave here, so what may be the purpose? I once asked him this question. It was years ago, but I still remember his response. He said: "I educate you so that you will be a better somebody in the future, and you may leave this house once you are ready."

I do not think I will ever be ready.

# VI

I am thankful I have a Grandpa, at least. I know it would have been impossible for me to live without him. With all his intolerable behavior, I still like him; I only hope that he will learn to be less angry and finds peace as well. I am still dealing with the ancient book, and unfortunately, it is not going well at all! I never thought that I would ever again need Grandpa's help, but I went to him today, while he was looking at a few books, and asked him for some assistance with one of the concepts in my book. I could not believe his response, though. He looked at the book blankly and was confused as well. Then he told me that he did not know the answer and suggested that he could borrow another book that may be more useful in answering my question. Knowing the types of books he would bring me, I refused and told him that I would figure it out by myself. But now that I look at it, I know I cannot.

# VII

Surprisingly, two weeks have already passed, and I have been in the process of finishing the book. Even though I do not have any other responsibilities other than studying and maybe sometimes cleaning around the house, the last two weeks have been quite challenging for me. I have been locking myself in my room and "Knocking myself on the head" in an exempt to try to understand what was being discussed in each section. Despite my tremendous efforts, it all seems hopeless. The concepts are too hard, beyond the limit of my brain to analyze and understand. Now, the problem is that my exam will be coming up soon. It is scheduled for Monday next week, which is only three days away! Usually, Grandpa gives me some time before asking me for the report and giving me the exam, but for this book, even though it is the most difficult, he has given me one less week time than he normally gives time for the other books. Interestingly, I am even losing the desire to learn as well. Not only have I been helpless, but I also think that there is not much more that I could do. Maybe I am very tired and need a very long and relaxing break, which I have not had for a few years now, or maybe I am getting lazy, as Grandpa believes.

I had mentioned the machine I have been building: It is almost ready. Based on my understanding on quantum physics and mechanics, and the necessary mathematical concepts which I have mastered through the years of constant studying, I believe that I have designed the correct Reverse machine. I have been working on this for years and in secret too, just like my writing, and have been making it using the excessive leftover lab materials from my lab work. I sometimes informed Grandpa of the certain necessary tools I needed by writing them on a piece of paper and making a list for him. He had routinely bought the items from the nearest possible location, so I am told. I believe the machine is ready, but I will have to recheck everything and test it to be sure.

# VIII

Today, while I was sitting at my window looking outside at the beautiful and ever-green grass, I thought about my stupidity over the years. Grandpa had been leaving me alone for a few hours, sometimes to go to the city, but I had been so stupid to have never left this house. I believe it was because I was scared, both of Grandpa and of the outside world. I remember how he always threatened me about the dangers outside of the house. Maybe now I will not be scared anymore. Maybe now I am ready to leave and face my destiny, whatever it may be. Oh, how I wish I could go out there . . . . Run barefoot on the green grass, smell the colorful, lovely flowers and just enjoy myself. But I do have to focus my thoughts now. The week has passed as quickly as it had arrived, and now I will have to face Grandpa and take my exam. I wrote a report as well, but because I did not understand most of the book, I had to come up with new ideas, which I am sure he will discover and become quite upset, but I really do not have another choice. At this point, I should just relax and hope for the best.

## CHAPTER 1

# The Truth

The weather had just started turning stormy, with dark, gray clouds covering the vast sky. Slowly, the wind begins to howl, and a piercing lightning strikes. It is Amy's heart that starts beating as hard as the willow tree branch is hitting the window of her room. She knows that this may be the time to fail, but she has no other options. She must obey her grandpa. She exits her room and heads toward the living room area, where Grandpa is patiently waiting for her at the table. The sky continues getting darker and darker until there are no traces of sunlight visible. Amy switches on the light and they both sit faced towards each other with the book placed in the middle. Grandpa started by taking a deep breath and reaching for the report. Amy also wanted to take a deep breath, but she felt as if she had no more breath left inside her body. She was afraid that if she had tried any harder, she would start choking for breath, which would look even more suspicious itself. After a few minutes of carefully looking through the report, Grandpa finally handed Amy two full pages of questions and asked her to begin.

Amy's heart started beating faster than ever, faster than she could ever imagine a human heart could beat. But because there was nothing else she could do at that point, she started answering the questions. The first few questions were easy and possible to answer, but as she progressed, the questions became more and more confusing to her. Towards the end of the exam, she was almost ready to cry! Grandpa noticed her strange behavior and asked her what was wrong. He even asked if he had given the wrong test to her, but Amy swallowed her sadness and claimed that there was nothing wrong. Finally, the time was over. Amy gave the paper back to Grandpa and left him alone, as he always asked her to do. Amy went to her room and started staring at the gray sky and at her favorite tree, the oak tree that reminded her of her parents, especially her father. She was very nervous, but she knew that being nervous would not be helpful at this point of time. It was already too late, and she knew she was going to be punished. This time, it could be by rewriting the whole book for twenty times or so. Who knows? Amy only sensed that Grandpa would not be happy with her, but she did not want to think about it because the more she thought, the more upset she became; therefore, she thought that the best action was to stay relaxed for the time being.

Amy's room was in no condition better than the weather either. It looked quite gloomy, with large books stacked on top of each other and posters of important and relevant scientific data on the walls of her room. It was much cleaner and more organized than other parts of the house, though, and felt much warmer than the computer room as well, but still felt lonely.

Finally, Grandpa opened the door while holding a few papers. He had the impression of being confused, but also amazed at the same time, and this scared Amy.

He asked, "Amy?" and she responded, "Yes, Grandpa?"

"Well, can you check your own work, please?" asked Grandpa.

"What? I mean, why do you want *me* to check on my own exam?" asked Amy, surprisingly.

"Well, because I think this way you will learn better, and I also trust you and am sure that you will not really change your actual grade," replied Grandpa.

Well, he was not entirely correct about changing the grade, Amy thought.

"Okay. I will check this, but Grandpa, you never allowed me to do this before. What happened?"

"Well, huh, I guess . . . oh . . ." answered Grandpa.

"Is something wrong?" asked Amy, patiently.

"No! Not at all. Why are you asking?" asked Grandpa.

"It's only that you have been acting strange recently, and if there is anything that I can do, you should let me know," responded Amy.

"Well, then, do what I told you and ask no more questions," demanded Grandpa.

But Amy was not satisfied. She felt that there was something Grandpa was hiding from her, something important, so she followed him to the living room and kept asking, "What's wrong?" and "What are you hiding from me?"

Amy thought that while she had been quite a handful to be raised, she did not want to cause any trouble, and most of the time, she tried to be kind to her grandpa. Also, she had been living with him for all these years, and she truly deserved to be told the truth about everything. But it was not easy making Grandpa do what he did not intend to; however, after hours of talking and convincing him to speak, he finally told Amy all he needed to say.

"Well?" asked Amy.

"Well, I cannot tell you. Please do not ask anymore," snapped Grandpa, angrily.

"But why? Have I done something wrong? Are you angry at me?" demanded Amy.

"No! Not at all. It's just that, oh, I . . . Okay. I must tell you. After all, you do deserve to know, but you should also know that I have been meaning to tell you this before, but the right time never came. The truth is that I cannot read, Amy," responded Grandpa.

"What?" Amy's world suddenly went all black. She could not believe it. All this time, Grandpa had been making her do all this tremendous amount of educational work and had been "checking on her," but how?

"Please do not be upset with me. I just thought that if I were to tell you the truth, you would have not trusted me and would have left me," said Grandpa.

"But I had nowhere to go. Where could I have gone after I had left you? It doesn't matter now. Just tell me what other secrets you have kept from me?" demanded Amy.

"Please don't say that! I tried my best to be a good Grandpa. Do you know how hard it was to educate you when I did not have any education myself? I had to bring all the books that had the solutions as well, and I just had to compare the looks of them and see if you were right," said Grandpa in a soothing voice.

"So, all this time, you have not been reading my reports either, just looking at them? Also, you can't be sure that all I have learned were correct information either, since I never had any help and you did not know how to check my answers. So, most of what I know is wrong," said Amy.

"No! I do not believe that. If you had studied everything, you should be a very knowledgeable person by now," replied Grandpa.

"Well, why are you telling me this now? I think it may be quite late, don't you?" asked Amy sarcastically.

"I had to tell you because I could not understand what that book was saying! Even by looking and comparing the answers I found nothing in common. So, I was afraid I was doing this wrong and asked you to check it for yourself," admitted Grandpa.

Well, Amy's exam results did not turn out as she was afraid to, but now, she felt even more devastated and disappointed than ever. She felt betrayed and deceived. She wanted to run, but she had nowhere to run to.

"Excuse me, Grandpa. I need to rest for now," murmured Amy.

"Of course. Amy?" said Grandpa.

"Yes?" replied Amy.

"I'm sorry," said Grandpa.

# CHAPTER 2
# The Walk

The wind kept on howling while Amy's heart kept on pounding. She could not imagine in her wildest dreams that someone as trustworthy as her grandpa could ever lie to her about such an important issue. She had spent about half of her life with him in his house, but he had always kept such secrets from her. The fact that all this time Grandpa could not even read seemed impossible to Amy. She knew deep down that he had done all this for her and her success, but by doing this, he had only ensured of Amy's failure rather than her success.

*Is this all real or am I really dreaming all of it? Is it true that by now more than half of all I know may be wrong?* Amy thought.

Now, Amy had no choice. She did not have the choice to take control of her own life since moving in with Grandpa. He had always been dictating her on what she should do and how she should do it.

The night was terrible. Amy could not even close her eyelids. Not only did the wind kept on howling and making the willow tree branch hit her window rapidly, but her thoughts about Grandpa kept interfering with her ability to sleep. Finally, the next morning came, and Amy dreaded leaving her room, for she was not looking forward to seeing her grandpa again. She still had difficulty understanding why Grandpa had kept such an important secret from her. As she was leaving her room, she heard someone pulling a chair along the floor. She peeked to see what was happening and was amazed by what she saw. Grandpa had been cleaning up the living room, and he was now preparing breakfast! Even though Amy was not happy with her grandpa, she was interested to see what had happened to him, for he had never done anything like this before. He used to leave the house every morning before sunrise, leaving a heap of new books and papers, along with a few dishes of food for Amy on her table. He would then return late in the evening, so exhausted that he would just collapse on the couch and take a long nap, or watch television.

*Maybe he doesn't have work today*, wondered Amy, but she decided to see what was happening, so she changed and started leaving her room. As she was approaching the living room, Grandpa stopped, turned around, and stared into Amy's eyes, and said: "Good morning, Sunshine." Well, this truly surprised Amy, who responded, "Good morning, Grandpa!" Of course, Grandpa was never used to speaking in kind words. He used to order everything and likewise never expected disobedience. However, Amy had accepted his behavior for a long time now. Even though Amy had not fully known her grandpa before moving in with him, she was convinced that it were the trauma from the war and the loss of his daughter that had made him turn into such a person. She always wanted to believe that deep down, Grandpa was indeed very nice and caring.

"Listen, I am truly sorry about last night and about everything else, but I am going to make it up to you," said Grandpa.

"You don't need to. Not anymore, but thank you for the offer," muttered Amy.

"No, no. You don't understand. I have called one of my oldest friends and have asked him to send me his grandson who is a very intelligent child, to come and help you with your educational goals. Now, I am sure that you will like his teaching, even though I believe that you will need none of it, but just to be on the safe side, I have asked him to come here. I think he should arrive shortly. Why don't you organize your room and start showing a more welcoming face?" suggested Grandpa.

"Oh, Grandpa. If you were really concerned with me, you would have thought about this sooner. Why didn't you find help for me earlier?" asked Amy.

"I was wrong. Very wrong. You see, I thought I could help you, but now I know that I am only an old, good-for-nothing Grandpa. I thought I would learn how to read and write from you later, and I have a little, but not enough to be of any assistance. Dear Amy, will you ever forgive me?" asked Grandpa.

Well, that was the very first time that Amy could remember Grandpa calling her "Dear," so she responded:

"Please let us not talk about this further. I need to take a walk. I assume it should be fine now?" asked Amy.

"Yes, of course. But you haven't eaten your breakfast yet. Surely they will come soon, so . . . ," said Grandpa.

"No, thank you. Grandpa, I'll be back soon," interrupted Amy.

"Okay, dear Amy. Please do not go far. Where are you going anyways?" asked Grandpa.

"Not far, only around here. Please do not ask any more questions," and she grabbed her Reverse machine and left.

This Reverse machine was the only real and loyal thing that Amy felt she had now. She knew that deep down, her grandpa did not really want to annoy her, but she could not imagine what he had done to her, keeping her in the ignorance all this time. She kept walking and walking and did not look back until she reached a wonderful cherry tree. She had read about them and had seen pictures of them, but the real tree was very beautiful and much more majestic. It was summer time and from the tree hanged hundreds of shiny, red, and perfectly round cherries. Amy hesitated, but she touched the tree trunk and then its leaves and the grass. Since the cherries were all ripened and ready to be picked, Amy reached for one as well.

"Hmmm. Amazing!" she said as she tasted a red cherry.

It felt just like before, just like when she was with her parents. She reached into her pocket and took out the Reverse machine. This was a small, round, metallic, dark tool with two long and metallic wires, with one that was supposed to be attached to the ground and the other that needed to be attached to the person's forehead. There were many little screws and holes around it that were needed for the creation of the appropriate circuit inside the machine. Amy took a deep breath, pictured her parents standing by her side smiling at her. She wished them back, and she connected the machine to herself and started it up.

## CHAPTER 3
# The Magical Land

$S$uddenly, the wind started howling through the trees and caused most of the leaves to fall off. The wind was so strong that it started to shake the trees violently and made standing quite uncomfortable. Amy looked down at her Reverse machine, and saw that it was vibrating wildly with a tremendous amount of force inside. But Amy had no choice now. She only looked up at the sky, but what she saw sent shivers down her spine. The sky was turning to a color she had never seen before. She had read about the different situations that could affect the weather, but never had she known about the existence of a green sky! It looked as if the wind had carried all the beautiful green leaves up to the sky and had caused it to turn green! While Amy was thinking about the sky and the other wonders of the universe, something hard knocked on her head, and she fell down, looking pale and motionless.

After a while, Amy tried to open her eyes slowly. She started looking around for her Reverse machine, but could not find anything, only a few pieces of broken and mangled metal pieces and ashes. Fighting tears, she decided to find out more about where she was, so she started looking around and found herself in a very strange place. It was a forest, but a very different forest than what she had expected. The trees blazed in completely different colors and forms, each being unique. Some were all orange, while others were pink, purple, blue, yellow, and red! The different trees, standing tall next to each other, dazzled Amy's eyes, creating a truly breath taking view. It was simply wonderful. Amy started walking down the path that was covered with the colorful leaves. Different colors started mixing together wherever she stepped. It felt just like magic!

*This land is magical! But where am I?* Amy wondered.

Looking around for an answer, she heard the galloping of a horse and quickly went to hide behind a blue tree nearby. She then saw a beautiful white horse, and on it, a strange looking person. As the person came down from the horse, Amy tried looking at him more closely to see who he was, but she could not see well because as soon as she was stretching over to have a better look, a follower ran towards him and led him to the opposite direction.

*Phew! That was close. I'm lucky he didn't see me. He looked quite strange. But who was he? Maybe he could help me find my way back home,* thought Amy.

She started following him, but as soon as she wanted to make the first move, the horse noticed and started neighing for his owner. Hearing the horse, the pair quickly came back running, and as soon as Amy heard their footsteps again, she quickly ran the opposite way. While she was running away, she fell into a deep hole that was covered up by the leaves, completely hidden from view.

"Oh, no! Hello, can you please help me?" shouted Amy.

She thought about how stupid she was to run away and how now, she had to ask for help! But immediately, a dark figure appeared above the hole and threw a long rope down to her.

"Oh, thank you very much!" sighed Amy.

As she was pulled out of the hole, what she saw scared her beyond limits. She was so afraid that she could not even speak. In fact, her smile was dried on her face, and no matter how hard she tried to say something, she was unable to move her lips! Amy's rescuer was a tall, relatively thin man with a very long hair that had strands of light green, golden yellow, and dark brown mixed altogether, and his ears looked sharp and were somewhat pointing outward. His clothes were similar to a very long robe that had a light green color, but showed rays of golden yellow in front of the sunlight, and had special patterns sewed on it. On his forehead was tattooed a sign that resembled a crown with a bright, green jewel on it. Despite his strange appearance, his face looked very kind and caring, but because Amy had never seen anyone with such a complexion, she was very frightened at first.

"Umm . . . ," Said Amy, after a while. "Wh-who are y-you?"

"Oh! English, right! Well, I am the Elf Land's Prince, of course! Surely, you must have heard of me?" said the Prince gently.

"Oh, right. Thank you very much for rescuing me," said Amy.

"Sure! My pleasure. Is there anything else I could help you with?" asked the Prince kindly.

"Well, I was hoping you would answer a few questions that I have," said Amy, while standing up to her feet.

"Sure. Anything," said the Prince.

"Well, could you tell me where I am? And how long is it to the village?" asked Amy.

"Oh, we are in Elf Land, of course! And I can lead you straight to the village. As a matter of fact, that is where we were going. Oh,

I forgot! This is my royal assistant, Sir Sunshine the Great," said the Prince.

Now, Sir Sunshine was very short compared to Amy and the Prince. He had a long, dark beard, but was wearing the same clothing as the Prince was. The only exception was that he did not have the tattooed sign on his forehead. Despite his strange appearance to Amy, his face looked quite calm and very kind. Even though Sir Sunshine was trying to show a welcoming face, Amy could not control her laughter anymore; she had to laugh at his name! Also, the Prince needed to sound casual, as to not offend either Sir Sunshine or Amy, so he just started laughing politely with Amy.

"Wow!" gasped Amy at Sir Sunshine.

"Oh! That does it! We'll leave right this instant!" said Sir Sunshine in a grumpy voice.

"No! I am so sorry! I didn't mean to hurt your feelings. Please. I need your help," said Amy.

"She's right, Sir Sunshine. We can't leave her here!" said the Prince.

"What? Oh, yes we can! See? I am leaving," and he took a few steps ahead, but sighed and returned, saying to the Prince, "You know I can't leave you here, so just please come with me and forget her," pleaded Sir Sunshine.

"*We* will come together," said the Prince firmly.

"B-but . . . Oh, fine. But young lady, please keep your thoughts to yourself," said Sir Sunshine in an angry voice.

"Right. I'm sorry. I did not mean to insult you. It's just that I had never seen anything this strange, yet amazing in my life! You see, I am not from around here and I was never allowed to come outside of our house either, but now that I did, I feel both happy and upset. Happy because I have seen some of the world now and have gained to my knowledge, but upset because I have left my grandpa alone suddenly," said Amy.

Hearing this made both Sir Sunshine and the Prince upset, so Sir Sunshine forgave her and they continued on their journey together.

# CHAPTER 4
# The Darkness

The prince held his hand for Amy to climb on the back of the horse, and together they rode through the enchanting forest, while Sir Sunshine was riding on his own, brown, smaller horse alongside the Prince. Now, the Prince's horse was all white, but had a light green mane, and on top of the horse's head a golden trinket was placed that resembled two pairs of wings. As Amy sat on the horse, she felt amazed to see the land under her own two feet; it felt that maybe, for once, she was in charge. While they were riding through the colorful trees, Amy could smell the scent of all the different flowers, which felt like there was a mixture of sweet chocolate, fresh berries, and roses in the air. She tried to find out from which direction the smell was coming from, but no matter how hard she tried, she could not understand the source of this wonderful scent. All around them were trees of beautiful and different colors that felt so soft to the touch. At a distance, the sound of a waterfall could be heard, and of course, the rustling sound of the leaves as they were proceeding through the forest added to the beauty of this magical place. Amy started remembering her parents and her grandpa again. She truly missed them and wished that there was a way they could be together again. Now, she was hoping that the kind people she had met would help her find her home again, for she knew she wasn't capable of living by herself in a strange, new land. It was an irrational and impulsive behavior to leave Grandpa, the only person who had cared for Amy all this time. The thought of home made her tears fall slowly down her cheeks. Meanwhile, the Prince was interested in finding out more about Amy, for she did not look at all like any elves he had ever seen before. So he started asking a few question from Amy:

"So, where are you from?" asked the Prince.

"The village," answered Amy.

"Oh, because I had never seen you there . . ." wondered the Prince aloud.

"I know. I was not allowed to leave the house," responded Amy.

"But why? Oh, I am sorry. It is none of my business. I apologize," said the Prince.

"No. It's alright. My Grandpa was a man who cared too much about me, but I only noticed this when it was too late . . ." said Amy quietly.

"I am very sorry," said the Prince, "but I am certain that you will see him again."

Amy tried to forget her sad thoughts and focus on the present, but it was hard. Whenever she closed her eyes, the image of Grandpa came into her mind, apologizing and being very upset. Finally, after Amy started controlling her tears. She noticed how the colorful leaves were losing their beauty and were becoming fewer and fewer in number as they were proceeding down the path. The leaves now started falling rapidly to the ground, and a chill tinged the air. Suddenly, Amy saw a dark figure flying very fast alongside the trees.

"What was that?" asked Amy.

"I didn't see anything," admitted the Prince.

"But I just saw it . . . There, that black thing that flew across . . . right there," commented Amy as she pointed towards the trees that were now almost completely bare.

Suddenly, the horse started whining and galloping very fast.

"What's happening?" asked Amy.

"I think I know where that dark figure is and I think it is following us. Just sit tight," commanded the Prince.

The horse was running so fast that it trembled over a log. He fell down hard and threw the Prince, Amy, and Sir Sunshine in different directions, knocking Amy and the prince unconscious, while Sir Sunshine was only slightly hurt. So, he quickly stood up and started running towards the Prince. But as he raced towards him, an invisible force pulled him down and made him fall. He quickly looked around and stood up again. The invisible force still pulled him down to the cold ground. This time, he got quite angry and called out: "Who is there? What do you want from us?"

Suddenly a gust of wind appeared from the sky and before him formed a gigantic black, hooded figure.

"W-what are you?" asked Sir Sunshine, holding his small dagger out.

"Hmmm. You have not heard of me? It does not matter. You and your friends shall all perish for entering my territory," said the dark figure in a deep and irritating voice that sounded like long nails scratching on a glass.

"Please! We were just passing by and meant no harm. Please spare us, and we will leave and never come back here again," said

Sir Sunshine in a shivering voice, while he was deliberately trying to avoid looking at the hooded creature's white, glowing eyes.

"Why should I spare you and your little friends? I have never spared anyone who dares to come here, now why should there be an exception?" asked the dark figure sarcastically while floating close to the ground.

"Oh, we will do anything you ask. Please, just allow us to leave here, and whatever you need in the future will be given to you at all costs," said Sir Sunshine.

"How can I trust you?" asked the dark figure.

"I shall give you my word and my name: Sir Sunshine the Great, so that you may claim anything you need in the future directly from me," muttered Sir Sunshine.

"Very well, then. I need you to promise me one thing on your honor: to bring back the girl for me after her journey is finished, but if you do not, I shall come back and hunt you and your little friends and make you regret you have ever been born," threatened the dark figure.

"T-the g-girl? Right! I will," said Sir Sunshine.

So, Sir Sunshine gave his word, and as soon as he swore to return with Amy, the dark figure left as quickly and mysteriously as it had appeared.

"My Prince? Please wake up!" urged Sir Sunshine frantically.

"Oh, what is it? What? Where? What happened?" asked the Prince hurriedly and confusingly.

"Nothing. We just have to leave. Now!" insisted Sir Sunshine.

"Very well then," said the Prince, and he went to pick up Amy, and they all headed out of the bare, gloomy forest.

## CHAPTER 5
# The Village

"Would you like to tell me what happened now?" asked the prince angrily because Sir Sunshine had been trying very hard to avoid explaining to them what had transpired with the dark figure.

"Well, yes. But we will need to keep going for now. It will be quite dangerous to stay longer in this forest," said Sir Sunshine.

"Very well. We are leaving, but I know that you are hiding something from me," said the Prince through clutched teeth.

So they continued riding through the bare forest amidst the dried, pointy trees and foggy air, and after a few hours, they finally arrived at the village. But, the journey had been so long that it had made Amy too tired, and she had fallen asleep on the back of the horse, leaning on the Prince.

"Alright. Here we are!" said the Prince joyfully.

Amy yawned and slowly sat tall on the horse. Before her laid a very beautiful place. There were many different people, each bustling around. Some were running around, and some were speaking to each other in a language that Amy had never heard of before. It sounded like a mix of all human languages that she had heard before, but was interesting and calming to listen to as well. The people looked more like the Prince rather than Amy, with pointy ears and colorful clothing. It looked like a lively and amazing city. The houses all differed in color. Each one was unique and looked very special. Some were in a square shape, while others looked like spheres, and some were oval shaped. As the group was riding through this wonderful place, the citizens started to halt on what they were doing and looked at the prince and his followers, the royal advisor, Sir Sunshine, and Amy.

"You must be a very great prince since everyone is looking at you with such awe," wondered Amy aloud.

"I would like to believe so," said the Prince kindly.

"This place looks wonderful! Where are we?" gasped Amy.

"Your village, of course, where you asked me to bring you," responded the Prince.

"Oh, but our village looks completely different than this place," said Amy.

"Well, this land is quite an immense place itself. Maybe your village is only a part of this place?" suggested the Prince.

"Maybe. I have never been out of the house, so I cannot be sure," said Amy.

"Don't worry. I am sure you will find your house," said the Prince.

"I hope so," said Amy.

While they were speaking, they were also making their way to the palace. It looked just like a fairy tale castle which was from a fairy tale book Amy used to read with her mother when she was younger. They used to read it every night together, so Amy remembered every minor detail about the fairy tales' castles, royalties, and the super-human creatures. Amy thought:

*What if I am in a fairy tale?* She used the Reverse machine, but what if the machine transported her to one of her best memories instead of actually turning back time? Maybe time was not reversed after all. But now what could be done? How could she come out of this memory? She was enjoying this land very much, but she needed to go back as well because she missed her home and her grandpa already.

The path to the castle was made with gray, large, but smooth stones. The colorful, majestic trees standing tall next to each other, with the same colors facing oppositely, added to the amazement of the palace's entrance view. The trees resembled the ones Amy had seen in the enchanted forest, but only they were even much more majestic here! As they were reaching the palace, Amy saw that the castle walls were all lavender in color, and all around it grew lavender and pink flowers. It was a breath-taking view! The smell of the wonderful flowers mixed with the fresh smell of soil, started filling Amy with joy. She looked around to see all the different, lovely creatures by the flowers. There were butterflies that looked quite different than any she had ever studied before. They were in a completely different color and had distinct patterns on each of their wings. One of the butterflies that landed on Amy's hand had one of its wings covered by green circles, while the other pair of its wings had purple swirls on it! After passing through the royal garden, Amy saw two short men, about three feet tall, with long, green beards, and light purple garments, each holding long spears in their right hands, poised in guard duty.

"Awe. They look so cute!" exclaimed Amy.

"What? Who said that? How dare you?" shouted one of the short men while pointing his spear towards no one in particular.

"Oh, I am very sorry! I meant no insult," said Amy.

"Oh. Your Elfship! Please forgive me," said one of the guards, while bowing low, and he stepped away to allow the Prince to enter.

"Thank you very much, Sir Moonlight," said the Prince.

"Sir Moonlight? Where do these names come from? They are not well matched to the characters at all," whispered Amy to herself.

Then, the prince gave his horse to Sir Moonlight and asked him to take it to the stables and tell one of the servants to care for it, and he led Amy inside the palace.

The inside of the palace looked even more enchanting than the outside! Each of the walls was green and purple with different patterns on them. The ceiling was covered with remarkable art work that resembled the nature, and especially the enchanted forest with the different and colorful trees and plants, and surrounding it a dark line was painted. As Amy looked more closely, she realized that the markings were not just an art work, but they were a language which Amy had never seen before.

"What is that?" asked Amy, pointing at the ceiling.

"That is the name of all our ancestors, the ancestor elves, and it is written in the elf language, which you may be unfamiliar with," responded the Prince.

"Right. It is wonderful! Like a complete life history under one roof!" said Amy, and they continued walking in the hall, covered with the green marbled floor, until they reached the throne room. Amy knew about royalties. She had read about them before both in her history courses and her novels, but this throne room was very different compared to the other ones she had read about before. The throne room's walls were all bright yellow in color, with a very large, golden chair placed at the center. Surrounding the throne chair were fourteen smaller golden chairs, with seven on each side, and a long table in between, with a red cover spread on it. Also, in front of each seat, a pile of papers were seen.

"What are the chairs for?" asked Amy.

"Well, those are the chairs of the royal advisers. There are fourteen of them, as you can see, and Sir Sunshine is one of them," answered the Prince.

Sir Sunshine who was walking along with them until now, started going towards his seat, which was on the right hand side next to the throne chair, and started looking at his papers.

"They help my father in solving problems and running the kingdom, so as you could imagine, they are almost always very busy," informed the Prince.

Amy could also see a bright yellow sign on the floor, before the throne chair, which was in a shape of a crown with a pair of wings attached to it. At the entrance door, there were two elf soldiers with their spears held high, wearing the same uniform as the guards outside of the castle. Suddenly, the soldiers moved to the corners of the room, and someone else entered the room as well. He looked like an elf as well, but was much taller than the other citizens and had a light purple cape and a golden crown with a green jewel in the center. He also had the same tattooed sign as the Prince had on his forehead, but looked colder and bitterer. He started walking slowly towards the central, high, golden chair, sat down and started staring at Amy's eyes.

"Hello, father," said the Prince casually.

"And who might this young lady be?" asked the Prince's father.

"This is Amy, Father. She had lost her way in the woods, and she needed help, so I led her to our castle. I am sorry I did not send any signals before coming here. We had an unfortunate event during our journey. Amy, this is my father, the King of Elf Land," said the Prince.

"And what might have been the unfortunate event?" asked the King immediately.

"Sir Sunshine knows more about it, Father. But he refuses to tell us," responded the Prince.

"Well then, in that case, welcome, Amy. You may take a room here and stay as long as you wish," said Eltor.

"Thank you very much, your Elfship, but I must find my own village soon. I am sure that my grandpa is devastated by now," said Amy.

"I am certain that Devdan will help you," said the King.

"Who is . . . ?" asked Amy.

"That is I," said the Prince before Amy could finish her sentence. "It is my real name, and you may call me by it, if you'd like," responded Devdan.

"Okay," said Amy. Since she never truly felt such a close intimacy before with anyone, she now felt quite happy and for once again close to someone.

At this, the King signaled one of the servants to come and show Amy to her room.

## CHAPTER 6

# The Friendship

$\mathcal{A}$s Amy was following the king's servant, who looked like a little plump, somehow short, lady elf, and was wearing a lavender apron, Devdan called her:

"Amy? Wait! You can't just go! I want to show you around," said Devdan hurriedly.

"Oh! Well, that's great! Can I just change quickly first, though?" asked Amy.

"Sure! I apologize for sounding a little rushed. Right, I will also change, but I'll see you in half an hour?" suggested Devdan.

"Right! I can't wait!' said Amy and she started going up the golden stairs, following the King's servant to the room.

Amy had thought that all the elves should have a green skin color, or at least be wearing all green and stay jolly and happy, but this was not necessarily true as she was seeing here at Elf Land.

"Now, the Prince asked me to meet him in an hour for a tour around the castle, but I don't really know how to prepare for this!" wondered Amy aloud that the King's servant also heard it.

"Oh, don't worry girl! I can help you if you want," suggested the King's servant kindly.

"Why, thank you. Yes, it would be great, if you would please help me. My name is Amy and I am from . . . not around here, I think," said Amy.

"I noticed that, Amy. My name is Mylaela, and I've been serving for longer than I can remember, dear!" said Mylaela.

"It is a pleasure meeting you, Mylaela. You said that you have been serving here for a very long time, correct?" asked Amy.

"Yes, dear," responded Mylaela.

"Well, then maybe you could help me! You see, I am looking for my village, and more importantly, my grandpa. I believe that we used to live around here, can you help me find my home again, please?" asked Amy.

"Well, dear. You will have to be much more specific with the directions to your house! You see, Elf Land is quite an immense place itself and it wouldn't surprise me if you could find many different villages and cities here, but be patient dear. I am sure that you can find your home again, but right now we need to get you ready for your tour with Devdan, right?" said Mylaela.

"Oh, you also call him by his first name?" asked Amy politely.

"Sure! I raised him myself, you know. Poor thing, he lost his mother when he was very young and since then, I chose to take a personal care of him. Of course, it was all under the supervision of the King, and Sir Sunshine who was also much younger back then, so Devdan and Sir Sunshine used to play together all the time! Oh, I miss those times!" sighed Mylaela.

"Wow! So much like my past. Only that I did not have anyone to be with, really," murmured Amy.

"Really? Sometimes we feel alone, but you know, we never are truly left alone. Do you know what I mean? Oh, well, don't worry!

Right now, we need to get you ready! Let's see, my goodness! You only have fifteen minutes left! Hurry, dear! Here, would you like this dress?" asked Mylaela while holding a long, light green velvet dress. The dress had a few red, shining gemstones on the center and had a wavy end to it as well that only added to the elegance of it.

"It's beautiful! More than I could ever hope for! But did you say you know the time?" asked Amy.

"Why, of course dear! You are asking strange questions, you know. As the palace's only headmistress of the servants, I am responsible to know almost everything! I will need to be able to speak different languages, know the rules, and the time too!" responded Mylaela.

"Right! But can I see a clock?" asked Amy.

"I don't know what you mean dear! But I know that you are getting late! Wear this now, please," insisted Mylaela, and she started helping Amy to wear the dress.

"Wow! You look dazzling! Wait until Devdan sees you! I know that he is quite a shy Prince, but he is very kind and always means well," assured Mylaela.

"I know. I need to properly thank him for saving my life too, when I fell into a deep hole. That's how we met!" explained Amy.

"A hole? You should be more careful, dear. There are many of them around here," said Mylaela.

"I will!" said Amy, laughing.

"Now, let's fix your hair, shall we?" asked Mylaela kindly.

"Thank you! I've never had anyone do my hair before! My mother used to braid it with me sometimes, but ever since she and my father passed away, my world has gone blank," said Amy.

"Well, it's my pleasure to do your hair! I always loved to raise a girl by myself, but I have never been able to obviously. Devdan was a very nice boy, but it's different raising a girl, you know?" said Mylaela.

"Thank you! I hope my grandpa would think the same way," said Amy quietly.

"Oh! You are late, dear! Hurry up now, but make sure to be back soon. I know you must be very hungry and tired, so I will prepare something suitable for you," said Mylaela.

Amy's long, shining, black hair was braided and tied on the top, and with her elegant dress, she looked quite different. For once in a very long time, she felt important.

"Sure. Thank you so much, Ms . . . ." wondered Amy.

"Call me Mylaela, dear! A friend of Devdan's is truly a friend of mine. Now off you go!" said Mylaela while leading Amy out of the room.

As soon as Amy started going down the stairs, she saw that Devdan was already waiting for her in a dark green coat and matching pants, holding a bouquet of colorful flowers. As Devdan saw Amy, his heart apparently skipped a beat. He stepped one step back and bowed down shortly before her! Seeing this caused Amy to blush a little, but since she also wanted to show the same respect, she also curtsied shortly as well.

"Well! You look radient! Are you ready?" asked Devdan.

"Thank you! And you too . . . I mean, you look handsome! You know, sorry!" said Amy.

"No worries! Mylaela, can you let my father know that we won't be back until dinner?" asked Devdan looking up at Mylaela who was still standing at the top of the stairs holding Amy's old clothes.

"Dinner time? Devdan? Where exactly are you two planning to go to? You know you are needed here as well, right? Plus, Amy is tired and hungry! What are you two planning to eat until tonight?" asked Mylaela worriedly.

"Don't worry!" said Devdan, while running out of the palace door with Amy following behind him.

"Wait! You little . . . ," shouted Mylaela, but it was already too late for the two had already left the palace.

"Mylaela, where did the Prince go?" demanded the King who had suddenly appeared behind her.

"Oh, your Elfship! They had left to see around the castle. That's all! The girl, Amy is new around here, and Devdan though that it would be a good idea to show her around while she is still here, looking for her grandpa," explained Mylaela.

"What?" shouts the King. "How dare does he leave without my permission? I am the King, aren't I? Maybe it's time to remind him who is in charge here," said the King through clutched teeth.

"Your Elfship, if I may? Please give him this chance. I beg of you! He had always been obeying your every bidding, but only this once please allow him to be free for himself," pleaded Mylaela.

"What do you mean, 'free'? Mylaeal, if it were not for your years of loyal service, you would not have been standing here right now! But fine! I will let it go by this time only. When Devdan returned, ask him to come and see me," ordered the King, and he left immediately to the throne room where all the royal advisors were already waiting, and upon the entrance of the King, all stood up and held their right hands high.

"Your Elfship, is the Prince coming?" asked one of the advisors.

"No! He had already left . . . Who knows where to!" said the King angrily, but continued: "We should start without him. He won't be back until tonight,"

All the royal advisors were suited in light purple robes and each had a pile of papers in front of them that apparently needed the King's attention.

"My loyal advisors, as you know, the repeated attacks of the "dark figure" had caused so many problems that is threatening the existence of this Kingdom. But I have now found out that the underlying problem is that the Kingdom is falling from inside rather than the outside attacks! We need to fix this right now, before it is too late, and I have a suggestion. Perhaps the one and only suggestion," said the King while walking alongside the table. "The Prince will need to be avoided the chance of ruling one day," said the King calmly.

"What? Why? How?" asked Sir Sunshine, as well as some other advisors, and this caused a great commotion in the throne room.

"Why do you suggest as such? To eliminate your only son the chance of ruling the Kingdom to glory and success? He has proven to be a very . . ." argued Sir Sunshine.

"Proven to be a good—for—nothing! He has no clue on ruling the Kingdom and never will! He will destroy everything I had built so far! And as royal advisors, I expect that you would understand and help your King follow his plan, right?" asked the King.

"Wrong! No offense, your Elfship. But we all think that you need to reconsider your thoughts!" declared Sir Sunshine, while all the other members of the court nodded in agreement.

"Huh—Really? Very well, then. I will speak with Devdan tonight, and we'll see if we can come to an agreement or not. In the meantime, inform me of the other situations or issues in the Kingdom," demanded the King, and the session officially began.

"Amy, come on!" said Devdan, running towards the palace's garden.

"I'm coming! Wait . . . for me!" shouted Amy, running towards Devdan, but because of her long dress and the green grass that were somehow starting to tangle around her feet, she fell down hard on her knees.

"Ouch!' moaned Amy.

"Oh! Amy? Are you alright?" asked Devdan, running back towards her and helping her stand up again.

"Yes. Thank you!" said Amy, rubbing her dress that was now already muddy.

"I'm sorry! Let us sit her for now," said Devdan, and he pointed towards a wooden bench nearby.

"Thank you!" said Amy, and they sat together at the bench.

"Huh! It's amazing!" gasped Amy, looking at the view in front of them, seeing the majestic castle walls, with the magnificent trees, different flowers, butterflies, and even colorful birds! As Amy was observing, she saw an injured, small, fluffy, green bird fall down hard a few steps from her! She immediately ran towards it to help. Seeing this, Devdan also followed Amy, and together they saw that the bird had broken its right wing and was unable to fly anymore.

"Oh! You poor thing. We need to help it, Devdan," said Amy worriedly.

"Look what I have!" said Devdan, and he pulled out a small, purple handkerchief from a small, brown bag he was carrying. He then started wrapping the bird's wing around it and gave it back to Amy.

"Thanks, Devdan," said Amy.

Devdan gestured his hand towards Sir Moonlight who was standing nearby tending to the royal flowers, and said: "Sir Moonlight, can you please carry this injured bird back to the castle and see that it is tended to and taken care of, please?"

"Of course, your Elfship," said Sir Moonlight, while taking the bird in his hands.

At this, Devdan turned towards Amy and asked: "Well, shall we continue with our tour?"

"Sure! Where are we going now?" asked Amy.

"Come! I want to show you our stables," said Devdan, and together they started running again.

"Here we are!" said Devdan, opening the stable's door and inside Amy could see more horses than she could count!

"There must be at least fifty different horses here!" commented Amy in awe.

"Fifty one to be exact! This one is called "Prince" and I think you've already met him," said Devdan, pointing to his horse.

"Yes!" giggled Amy.

"Here! I have always left this for . . ." declared Devdan, pointing towards a beautiful, light pink horse with a golden mane. "Of course, if you'd like to try riding with me . . ." suggested Devdan.

"You must be joking, Devdan! I don't know how to ride," said Amy quietly.

"Don't worry! I didn't know either, but I learned. It is very entertaining! You should try, and I promise to help you," assured Devdan.

"Very well, then. What is it called?" asked Amy.

"Her name is "Princess", and she is very gentle," explains Devdan.

"Well, that's good to know!" said Amy.

"Come on! You can touch her if you'd like!" said Devdan and he held Amy's right hand and placed it on the horse's mane.

"It feels so soft!" commented Amy.

"Come on. Let's ride!" said Devdan, while leading a black, strong looking horse out of its stall, but as soon as Devdan's original horse, the "Prince" saw this, he started neighing so loud and kicked the stall's door open!

"Wow! I see that someone's a little jealous!" said Devdan, laughing, "But 'Prince', you must be very tired now. You must rest!"

But "Prince" was still not satisfied. This time, he started walking towards Devdan and neighed again!

"Very well, then. If you can manage . . . ," said Devdan, while leading the other horse back to its stall.

"So, how do I get on the 'Princess'?" asked Amy.

"Easy! Here, let me help you," said Devdan, while holding Amy's hands and helping her get on the horse.

"Wow! It feels great! Can we ride it out? I mean, of course . . . ," wondered Amy aloud.

"Sure! Come on 'Prince'," said Devdan while sitting tall on his horse.

"Now, Amy, sit tight and hold on to the 'Princess', okay?" asked Devdan.

"Right! But . . . ," started Amy, but before she could finish, the two had already started galloping out of the stable and were already out into the open again.

"Ahhh!" shouted Amy.

"Are you okay?" shouted Devdan back.

"I . . . don't know!" answered Amy.

"Sit straight, but hold tight! That's all you need to know!" instructed Devdan.

"Okay," sighed Amy, who was feeling amazed by now. She had no clue that riding could be so much fun! While running out, the light breeze started to flow down towards Amy's hair and brought the fresh smell of the wonderful flowers with it.

"The 'Princess' is magical!" exclaimed Amy.

"Of course! What did you expect?" responded Devdan, winking at Amy. "Ready for a race, Amy?"

"What? I mean, I can't!" sighed Amy.

"It's easy! Just close your eyes and believe! Come on, please?" asked Devdan.

"Very well!" responded Amy, while taking a deep breath.

"Ready? Whoever reaches that blue tree first wins, okay?" said Devdan.

"Alright!" responded Amy. "Come on, girl! You can do it!"

"No! *You* can do it, Amy!" responded Devdan, and the two started leading their horses towards the blue tree.

Devdan who was already ahead of Amy turns back to see her, but suddenly his horse halts and throws him forwards, and Devdan lands into the blue tree itself!

"Oh, No! Are you alright, Devdan?" asked Amy, running towards the blue tree.

"Huh, yes. I am fine, thank you. 'Prince'? What's wrong with you?" shouted Devdan from the top of the tree, and in response his horse only neighed back and walked away!

"Maybe he is tired. Devdan? Can you climb down yourself?" asked Amy.

"Climb?" asked Devdan. "You mean, jump?" and he suddenly jumps on the ground and uses his right hand as a support.

"Well, I think that's enough of the race, don't you?" asked Amy, giggling.

"But who won, then?" asked Devdan, scratching his head.

"Well, you landed *in* the tree first. But I properly rode until here, so of course, I won!" declared Amy.

"But it was all the 'Prince's' fault! I'm going to have a serious talk with him now!" teased Devdan.

"Come on, can we rest for now?" asked Amy, who was feeling quite hungry as well, since she had nothing to eat for a while now.

"Of course. Come, Amy. I'll show you to a very special place!" said Devdan, "But before we leave, we will have to tie these two friendly horses to this tree," and he pulled out a pair of long ropes from his small bag attached to the saddle on his horse, and started tying them to the blue tree.

"Come on, Amy. Follow me!" said Devdan while running past the blue tree.

"I'm coming!" replied Amy.

Behind the tree was an amazing area that was hidden from the view by the strands of willow tree all around it. Inside, Amy could see a small, dried fountain with a statue of a small boy standing inside. All around it were red flowers that looked very much like roses, and behind the fountain was a wooden swing.

"How wonderful! Where are we?" asked Amy.

"This is where I used to come when I was much younger. Sir Sunshine and I used to sit and play here by the water fountain, roll around in the grass, and even swing together! It is the only treasured memory I have from my childhood," explained Devdan, while sitting down at the swing. "My mother ordered this statue and the fountain to be made here. Later, Sir Sunshine and I made this swing and arranged the willow tree branches in a way to conceal our "secret hide-out". It has been such a long time, but you have no idea how much I miss living like that! Free to do whatever I want to do, whenever I want to do it! But after my mother passed away, my father started acting strangely. For one, he banned me from seeing or playing with Sir Sunshine again. I don't know why, but he never trusts me anymore, yet I have done nothing to disappoint him . . ."

"Devdan, I know what you mean," said Amy while walking towards him. "My grandpa has done the same to me, in a different way, I mean. I was never from the royalty, but I can understand why you're upset because I have lost both of my parents in a traumatic accident, and ever since then, I was supposed to live with my grandpa who had done nothing but banning me from everything! I, too was supposed to stay day after day in my room, studying and studying some more! And at the end, I found out that all this time, he could have never read! I understand that he meant well, but he certainly could have been more honest and open to me. Devdan, all I am trying to say is that maybe you should give your father another chance. Maybe it's the loss of your mother, or the pressure from the Kingdom that is bothering him? Maybe you could help him?"

"That's right," grunted Devdan. "My mother was the true royalty. She knew how to run a Kingdom, but I can't say the same for my father! Furthermore, he always refuses help. Even his most loyal advisors have a hard time persuading him of anything,"

"But you know, I really think that *you* can help him," responded Amy, but while Amy was speaking, suddenly, her stomach starts grumbling!

"Oops! How embarrassing! Sorry," said Amy, while holding her stomach tightly.

"Oh, no, no! I am sorry. Here, you should try some of these!" said Devdan, while taking out a small bag with some green and purple round, but soft food that looked like bread pieces or cookies to Amy.

"Oh, thank you! Are they safe? I mean, for me . . . you know . . ." asked Amy.

"Of course! I specifically brought them for you! Here, try some!" replied Devdan, and he ate one of the purple ones himself, and so Amy tried one of the purple ones as well. It tasted just like a mixture of cabbages, with carrots, onions, eggplants, and hot, red peppers!

"Wow! This is truly . . . amazing. What is this?" asked Amy while trying very hard to swallow.

"It's everything in one piece! All the nutrients one needs! This is really the traditional elf food," answered Devdan. "Wait, you don't like it, do you?"

"No! What makes you say that?" answered Amy with her mouth full.

"Because you are turning green, and apparently cannot swallow that! Here, try drinking some of this! It will help," said Devdan, and he gave Amy a bottle of what looked like water.

"Thanks!" said Amy, and without hesitation, she drank all of it.

"Wow! Oh! I think I feel weird!" commented Amy.

"Really? Like light headed and confused? That's normal," said Devdan, and he continued by asking: "Tell me, Amy. Why and how did you come here?"

"Well, I have always been dreaming of having my parents back, even if it meant for one day. So, I had been working on a very complex machine that was supposed to be capable of turning back time and perhaps bringing my parents back to life!" responded Amy.

"Wow! That is a genuine thought. I assume that it didn't work the way you wanted, right?" asked Devdan.

"I don't know what to say, Devdan. I knew it would have never worked anyways. I just wished that it would," sighed Amy.

"Uh, Amy, I think we should go now. It is getting late, don't you agree?" asked Devdan.

"Yeah. We should go. Devdan?" asked Amy.

"Yes, Amy?" answered Devdan.

"Thank you for everything," said Amy, and they both rode out towards the castle.

## CHAPTER 7

# The Plot

"Here we are! What a day, right?" asked Devdan, while getting off his horse and leading it back to its stall.

"It was amazing. Thanks again, Devdan," sighed Amy.

"Listen, I promise to help you find your grandpa tomorrow. I just needed my father's map, but since he was in the meeting all day long today, I wasn't able to ask for it. Amy?" asked Devdan.

"Yes, Devdan?" replied Amy.

"Do you think we could do this again tomorrow? After finding your grandpa, of course. We could see inside the castle, if you'd like," suggested Devdan.

"Sure! I would love to," responded Amy politely.

"Alright then! Let us not waste any more time! I'm starving!" commented Devdan, and they started walking out of the stables.

"Devdan? Come here!" whispered a familiar voice.

"Who was that?" asked Devdan, looking around the castle doors.

"Here!" repeated the voice, and this time she waved her hand at Devdan.

"Mylaela! What's wrong?" asked Devdan, running towards Mylaela who was standing in a small room in front of the castle's entrance door.

"Devdan, be careful! Your father is furious at you. Sir Sunshine and others are trying to calm things over, but I think you should proceed with caution," warned Mylaela.

"How do you mean? What wrong did I do?" demanded Devdan.

"I don't know, dear. But the King was upset that you did not show up for today's meeting, and I have heard that he had also made some shocking comments about you," explained Mylaela.

"What? He never told me I was supposed to be at the meeting today! Why can't he just . . ." started Devdan, when Amy, who was standing at the door all this time, asked if everything was okay.

"Yeah! Don't worry, Amy. I'll see you in an hour for dinner," answered Devdan and left angrily towards the throne room.

"Mylaela, is everything okay?" asked Amy.

"Yes, dear. Don't worry. We should get you ready! Come on, follow me," said Mylaela, and she started going up the stairs towards Amy's room, as Amy started following her.

"So, how did everything go? Oh, goodness! What happened to your dress, dear?" asked Mylaela, pointing to the muddy portion of Amy's dress.

"Oh, Mylaela, I fell down! I am so sorry. I can wash it myself," said Amy.

"Nonsense child! I'll take care of it for you. Here, would you like to wear this now?" asked Mylaela, holding a bright red velvet dress.

"Wow! It is so beautiful, and they are all the right size for me! How did you manage?" asked Amy.

"You see, dear, the queen had tons of clothes, but she never got a chance to wear all of them, of course, since she passed away so soon . . . And interestingly, you are the same size as her!" said Mylaela, laughing.

"I'm sorry about the queen. You really miss her, don't you?" asked Amy.

"Of course, dear. Who wouldn't? She was the sweetest, but the most determined ruler the Elf Land had ever seen. Pity she passed away so soon because of that wretched disease," explained Mylaela.

"What is the disease called, Mylaela? Do you know?" asked Amy.

"Be careful, child! We do not speak of its name anymore. It is believed to bring bad luck to the land! Anyways, a long time has already passed, and we have tried to let it go. So, where were we with your preparations? Oh, yes. Your hair! Maybe you should put your hair down this time, what do you think?" suggested Mylaela.

"I completely agree with you. My head had started feeling funny and I think it would be a good idea to change my hairstyle as well," responded Amy.

"Well, then. Here we go. Do you like it?" asked Mylaela after arranging Amy's hair down.

"Wonderful! Thank you so much, Mylaela," gasped Amy.

"Don't mention it, dear. Here, these are your clothes I had washed for you," said Mylaela, while handing Amy's old clothes to her.

"A million thanks, Mylaela," said Amy.

"You're welcome, dear. Now, we still have some time left. Why don't you rest a while, and I will send someone upstairs to accompany you to dinner soon," suggested Mylaela.

"Of course, Mylaela," responded Amy, and at this Mylaela left Amy in her room.

This room had a large, white bed, with a pink makeup and mirror set at a corner. On the walls were several paintings of the enchanted forest and the castle. Suddenly, Amy saw a door, which she hesitated to open, but she thought: *It's really none of my business! I should avoid being such a nosy girl! But if this did not concern me, then why is it in the room given to me?* And she decided to open this door anyways.

"Wow! How wonderful!" gasped Amy, for she could see what looked like an endless closet, full of colorful dresses and gowns. Some of the clothes had sparkles on them and some were very colorful and bright, but they all had a sign on the back. It was the same sign tattooed on the Prince's forehead before, a golden crown with a green jewel on it.

*I'm sure they were all from the queen. How sad that she passed away in such a traumatic way!* Thought Amy, and she went back towards the bed and lied down to rest.

"Father?" asked Devdan, knocking on the door to the King's private room, where you could find nothing, but stacks of papers all around the place, and the King sitting behind the desk.

"Come in, Devdan," answered the King, and Devdan slowly opened the door and sat on the empty chair in front of the King's.

"Mylaela told me that you wanted to see me?" asked Devdan.

"Yes," responded the King, looking through his papers at Devdan. "Can you explain to me where you wondered off to today?" demanded Eltor.

"I went to show Amy around the castle . . ." started Devdan.

"How dare you leave without my permission? And leave with a stranger? She could have been a criminal, or even worse, a spy in disguise!" argued the King.

"What do you mean? She was lost in the forest. I couldn't have just left her alone!" complained Devdan.

"Of course you could have! Look, you had left me alone today, didn't you? I see that you are capable of doing such a thing, but no, your family's safety is the only thing that doesn't matter to you, isn't that right?" asked the King.

"What family? Ever since mother had passed away, I had been left alone! You were never there for me," answered Devdan.

"I was busy ruling the Kingdom! What did you expect? Plus, you had Mylaela and Sir Sunshine," replied the King.

"Whom you banned me to see. Remember, father? You thought that Sir Sunshine was having a bad influence on me. You never realize what you've done!" shouted Devdan.

"Well, that certainly didn't stop you from seeing him again, did it?" asked the King sarcastically.

"What is your point, father?" asked Devdan impatiently.

"The point is that the girl, Amy is dangerous to you and she will have to leave right away!" demanded the King.

"What? But she is just a harmless, lost, young girl, and I have promised to help her find her grandpa again! You just can't be serious!" argued Devdan.

"Very well, then. You must avoid her from this moment on, until she is gone. Do you understand?" demanded the King.

"I can't understand your worries, but since I will need your map to help Amy, I have no choice, but to obey you," sighed Devdan.

"The map? Of course! I shall give it to her myself. Devdan, you will have nothing more to do with her from now on, do you understand?" said the King.

"If you insist. As long as she is safely returned back home, I have no complains," said Devdan, and at this one of the servants knocked on the door and announced that dinner was ready.

"I will be watching you, Devdan. And if you make one wrong move, your little friend will be gone," whispered the King to Devdan.

"Very well!" responded Devdan, and he left the room. While walking towards the dining area, he suddenly remembered a very special treasure given to him by his beloved mother.

*Of course. The mirror! But where could it be? Maybe Mylaela would know. I should ask her after dinner.*

While the King was thinking:

*Stupid boy! He will interfere with all my plans, I just know it. I will have to stop him, though. Even if it means by getting rid of him.* "Hello? Amy, dear?" called a familiar voice.

"Huh! Yes . . . Mylaela!" said Amy, yawning.

"Were you sleeping, dear? I'm sorry, but dinner is ready. Come now, I will have to fix your hair again," sighed Mylaela.

"Oh, I'm sorry. I don't know what happened to me. I just felt so light headed and had to sleep," explained Amy.

"Don't worry, dear! Here, you are ready. Before you go, dear, there are things that you need to know: Don't sit next to the King, don't speak unless spoken to, and don't eat unless the King allows for it," explained Mylaela.

"Thank you, Mylaela, but are the rules always this strict?" asked Amy.

"Yes, only now they are going to be even stricter!" said Devdan who had entered the room since the door was open. "Listen Amy, my father had decided to personally help you find your Grandpa. He had also demanded me to stay away from you! Who knows why! So, I just wanted to let you know that if I sound cold, it's because of this and nothing else. I truly enjoyed spending the day with you and I will always remember you. Amy, if I didn't see you again, well, this is for you," and Devdan, and he offered a small, black velvet box to Amy: "My gift to you, Amy. It was from my mother, the Queen, and I had kept it all these years, but I want you to have it now, and keep it as a memory from me and from here," said Devdan.

"I will. Thank you so much, Devdan," said Amy, and she opened the box and saw what looked like a pure diamonds necklace!

"Amy, can you wait for us for a minute outside?" asked Devdan politely.

"Sure!" replied Amy and she left the room.

"Devdan, dear! Maybe it is time for you to question your father?" suggested Mylaela.

"I tried, but he threatened me, and not me directly, but Amy's life! Mylaela, do you remember the mirror my mother gave you before she passed away?" asked Devdan.

"Yes, of course! I have kept it for you all these years. Do you need it now, Devdan?" asked Mylaela.

"I'm afraid, yes, Mylaela. Can I see you after dinner tonight?" asked Devdan.

"Sure, dear. Meet me in front of your room," said Mylaela, and she went to accompany Amy, who was standing a few feet away from the room to the dining area. Walking down the stairs, Amy started remembering her grandpa again. She knew that she needed the King's help in order to find her home. At the same time, she was worried about what would happen with Devdan and the King. Looking up, she saw Devdan standing at the top of the staircase, staring at the ceiling. She wondered what had caused the King to decide that Devdan be separated from her.

*Had I done something wrong? If so, how can I fix my mistakes now?* Wondered Amy.

Arriving at the dining area, Amy saw a far-reaching table, with a red tablecloth covering it entirely. There were exactly seven red, velvet chairs designed all around the table, and Amy could see more than ten different types of food! There were dishes that looked like vegetables, but each had a different color to it. Some were green, pink, light purple, sky blue, or yellow! There was also a large basket of the traditional Elf food that Amy had tried before with Devdan.

*Hmm. I know I will not try that "traditional food" again! But I wonder how the other food taste like. Back home, we used to eat almost the same type of food everyday, but here, it's so much more colorful!* Amy thought.

"Amy, dear, you could sit here," said Mylaela, pointing to a chair one seat away from the King's, whose chair was at the head of the table.

"Thank you, Mylaela," responded Amy.

As soon as Amy sat down, Sir Sunshine and Devdan also entered the dining area, and Sir Sunshine sat in front of Amy, while Devdan took the seat next to him. Looking at Devdan, Amy could see that he was indeed very upset. His green, shining eyes had now lost their happiness, and he had an expression of being both disappointed and angry. At this, two other elves that looked somewhat taller than the rest of the citizens and were completely bald entered the dining area as well. Following the two, the King dressed in a blue cape came towards the table and took his seat, while the other two elves sat next to him on the two other chairs positioned next to the King's. Then, Mylaela sat down next to Amy and the King started by gesturing his right hand towards Devdan to signal the start of the meal, and he started by tasting one of the purple traditional food, that Amy had also tried before.

"Very well. You may begin," ordered the King.

"Is the meal pleasing, your Elfship?" asked Mylaela.

"It is acceptable, Mylaela," answered the King.

Amy was not sure what to try, though. She looked around the table and there were all new food that she had never tasted before, but at the same time, she was worried that she would have the same prior experience with the "traditional Elf food." However, she was very hungry and wanted to eat something, so she glanced at

Mylaela and Devdan's plates, and they were both having the green and sky blue vegetables, so Amy started reaching for some as well.

*Hmm. This is much better! It tastes just like pomegranates, grapes, and oranges!* thought Amy.

"Is everything alright, Amy?" asked the King.

"Yes! Your Elfship. Everything is great!" answered Amy, surprised.

"It's good to hear this, for tomorrow we'll send you off to your grandpa," responded the King.

"Thank you, your Elfship," answered Amy kindly.

The Prince who was already annoyed, started reaching for his glass of water and then, glanced at the two elves sitting by the King, and asked: "Father? Will you introduce your guards to us?"

"Very well, Devdan! You understood correctly. These are my new, two personal guards, who will from now, dine with us as well," informed the King.

"May I ask the reason for this? We had always been dining together, without the interference of two other strange guards!" said Devdan boldly.

"Yes, but we had never dined before with the presence of a strange girl either!" said the King sarcastically.

"If you mean, me, your Elfship . . ." started Amy, but Devdan interrupted her: "No! Father? May I speak with you in private?" asked Devdan.

"Don't you see we are at the dinner table, Devdan? You could speak to me later," said the King coldly.

The meal was served with great sorrow for both Amy and Devdan, who at the end thanked the King and left to their rooms.

*How could I be strange? I have never done . . . Of course! I'm not an elf, so maybe that's what the King meant and I only misunderstood,* thought Amy. "Devdan, dear? Come! I found what you were looking for! It was in your mother's room all this time! You know, I never reorganized it again," said Mylaela, while standing at Devdan's door.

"Thank you, Mylaela. Have a good night," said Devdan, and he took the mirror that was wrapped in paper with him.

"You too, Devdan. Promise me to be careful," said Mylaela.

"I will be careful. Please don't worry," said Devdan, and he went to his room and locked the door, and Mylaela also left.

## CHAPTER 8

# The Secret

The next day, Amy woke up with a sound of bells ringing very close by. She stood up, looked around the room, and she remembered what had happened the day before: her grandpa, and the King's promise of helping her. So she quickly dressed up in her old clothes to be ready, and went downstairs. As soon as she reached the bottom of the stairs, Amy saw the King, who asked her to join him for breakfast! Amy had no choice, so she accepted the king's offer, and together, they sat at the royal breakfast table. The breakfast consisted of many, many different kinds of food. There were breads that looked like different shapes of animals, and also had different colors, as usual. The majority of them were purple and green, though. There was also what looked like some green jam and honey and a pair of boiled, purple eggs that were already prepared on Amy's plate.

"I specifically ordered these types of food, for I knew you would be more interested in them than our traditional Elf food, correct?" said the King, laughing.

"Sure. Thank you very much," responded Amy politely, and she started tasting one of the eggs. "Wow! It tastes wonderful!" gasped

Amy. She thought that it tasted just like the eggs her mother used to cook for her for breakfast sometimes.

"Hmm. You know, I have scheduled a great afternoon for us together in the royal garden. Devdan told me how much you enjoyed seeing around, and I am sure that you will enjoy it even more when you see our *special,* personalized royal garden," said the King joyfully.

"I would enjoy seeing your garden very much, sire, but I do need to leave. I need to find my Grandpa . . . ," said Amy.

"Sure, you will, but not right now! You must join me for your tour to the royal garden. I insist, as this is a part of our tradition for any visitor!" explained the King.

"Very well, but there is one condition," said Amy.

At this, the King's face turned red with anger, but he was deliberately trying his best to avoid showing this.

"Very well, what would that be?" asked the King.

"You must help me find my grandpa after our tour," insisted Amy.

"Sure", said the King through clutched teeth because no one had ever told him that he "must" do anything, and now this child dared to be so insulting to him, but he took a deep breath and held his feelings in check for he did not want Amy to suspect anything.

After breakfast was served, the King told Amy that he needed to get ready for the outdoor visit and asked her to do the same.

While Amy was walking up the stairs, she started wondering about King's strange behavior. She remembered his last night's behavior and it clearly did not match today's. He was acting quite complicated. For one, he did not sound very focused. He continuously turned red with anger, and he seemed to be quite interested in her, which was a frightening thought because no matter the social standing, she could not imagine living with elves! They are a group of different creatures and look and behave differently than humans do. She also thought about the absence of the Prince for the breakfast. As she was thinking, Devdan suddenly appeared before her.

"Oh, hello. Where were you?" asked Amy.

"At the breakfast table! How about you?" asked Devdan.

"What do you mean? I was at the breakfast table with the King, and you were not there," said Amy.

"Wait. Did you say the King? You were with him this morning?" asked Devdan.

"Yes, and he also asked me to join him for a visit to the royal garden today," said Amy.

"What do you mean? I am very confused. Even *I* am not allowed to have breakfast with him, let alone walk with him. No, no. You cannot go! You simply must not," and he ran down the stairs.

"Okay! I will wait then . . . Or maybe, I will get ready," wondered Amy aloud.

She thought that the King may be the only one who would be able to help her, and all she needed to do was to see the royal garden with him in order to receive his help, which she enjoyed as well. Once Amy entered her room and opened the closet, she saw that there was a shirt and its matching pants already hanging at the front, ready for her, so she quickly changed again, but also took the necklace that Devdan had given her the night before, since she thought that it was a precious treasure, then she went downstairs. As soon as she reached the bottom of the stairs, she saw the king all ready, dressed up in clothes that matched Amy's! The king looked quite handsome in them, and Amy could not help but smile at him. Still, she focused all her thoughts on her grandpa. She needed to find him, and nothing else seemed to matter to her at the moment.

"Well, you look very beautiful. Are you ready?" asked the King.

"Of course, your Elfship. Um, can I speak with Mylaela before we leave, though?" asked Amy.

"First of all, please do not call me 'your Elfship'. My name is Eltor. As for Mylaela, she was feeling unwell today, so she will not be able to assist you any longer. If you needed anything, my other servants will kindly serve you," replied the King.

"Oh, okay. I hope she feels better," said Amy, also thinking about the close level of intimacy she had obtained with Devdan and now the King!

"Very well, let us leave then," said Eltor, and as they were walking out of the door, Devdan came in running.

"No! Wait. Father? May I please have a word with you?" asked Devdan.

"No. I am in the middle of an important meeting. Later, perhaps," responded Eltor casually.

"An important meeting? What do you mean? Well, if you are not to talk to me in private, then I must tell you now!" demanded Devdan.

"Oh, alright. Please excuse me," said Eltor to Amy.

"What is it?" demanded Eltor.

"Father, may I ask what you are doing? Why are you taking Amy to the royal garden and our personal garden, as well? I know very well, as you do, that we have lost so many lives there. No offense, Father, but what do you want from her?" asked Devdan.

"It is not what I want from her, son, but what she wants from me that matters. She needs my help, and I do not even know what you mean by the loss of many in our garden?" whispered Eltor to Devdan, and he started walking towards Amy.

"You know very well what I mean. All the humans who disappeared there and were never seen again?" questioned Devdan loudly.

Amy was startled to hear this, so she asked Eltor what Devdan meant by the "disappearances."

"Nothing, Amy. Devdan had simply had a bad night and is not feeling well. It is an Elf condition, just like Mylaela's," muttered Eltor to Amy.

"But he seemed to be well this morning," responded Amy.

"Oh, so you have seen him this morning? Very well, he will be alright soon, but we need to leave now," said the Eltor.

"Right," replied Amy.

"Then I shall come with you as well, or I shall tell her everything," insisted Devdan.

"Tell me what?" asked Amy.

"Nothing important, probably about his illness," said Eltor, and he continued "Very well. You shall come as well. But remember, no weapons. We are going to enjoy ourselves," said the King.

"Right," said Devdan.

And they started walking towards the royal garden.

## CHAPTER 9
# The Return

$\mathcal{A}$s they were walking out of the palace, Amy started questioning herself. She looked at Devdan and saw that he was both very upset and angry, just like last night. She thought that maybe they were hiding something from her, a secret perhaps, but then again, she thought:

*What secrets could there be?* She barely even knew them, so why should she even care? But the King's behavior was also very strange. He kept looking at Amy precisely every ten steps and kept smiling at her. Also, Amy never knew that other "humans" had already been to this place! She thought that she was the only one who had traveled here, using her Reverse machine, but apparently she was mistaken.

Finally, they reached the royal garden. Oh, this place was amazing! Very much like the entrance view of the palace Amy had seen the day before, only more complete with all the different types of flowers she knew and did not know, and many butterflies and bees with different colors. To her left, were a group of pink, orange, red, and yellow flowers, and to her right, were a group of purple, blue, green, and a single black flower. In the middle of the garden of flowers was a stone pathway that had strange markings engraved on it, and in the center of all, stood a statue of a tall, caped and crowned man, holding two balls in one hand. Water was coming out of his other hand, as this was both a statue and a water fountain.

"Here we are. We could rest here for a while if you'd like," offered Eltor.

"Yes, but may we also see the personalized section of your garden?" asked Amy, who was more in a hurry of returning home by now.

"Of course! It is right over there," said Eltor, pointing straight into the wall.

"But I do not see anything there," admitted Amy.

"Well, of course not, because it is covered and secured," responded Eltor. "We will go there as well, but after we sit here and enjoy this scenery first."

Suddenly, out of nowhere, a large, gray stray wolf appeared next to the entrance of the "King's personal garden." Seeing the obviously hungry wolf scared Amy very much and she jumped up from her seat, but as soon as she wanted to escape, the king shouted, "Halt! If you try to escape, he will attack you. Just stay calm. Devdan, you usually carry weapons with you, even though I urge you not to. Can you do anything?" asked Eltor quietly.

"Well, I do. Just stand back," said Devdan and, he led Amy behind him. However, the wild wolf charged towards him at once, but Devdan chased it out of the garden.

"Oh, my! We need to warn the guards! Will he be alright?" asked Amy worriedly.

"Please do not worry about him. He'll be fine. He was trained after all. Let us continue our tour now," said Eltor calmly.

"What? I mean, your only son is dealing with a wild wolf, and you expect to have fun! How?" shouted Amy.

"As I said, you need not worry about him. He shall be fine. Now, I would like to show you my personalized garden," demanded the King.

"No! I am going after him," said Amy, but as soon as she tried to leave the entrance door, a gust of dark wind blew at her feet and disabled her to walk anymore. In pain, she turned around and saw the King's angry eyes glowing white at her. It was a very frightening scene, with many dark clouds in the sky covering the entire land. The sky kept growing darker and darker, and the wind started screaming through the trees. One by one, the flowers and beautiful trees lost their leaves, and shortly after, the whole garden was very dark. Suddenly, Amy felt that she was floating in midair, and as she looked around, she saw Eltor staring at her with his white, glowing eyes. The whole world spun wildly around her.

At the same time, Devdan who was fighting with the wolf, heard a very terrifying cry, and at this, the wolf disappeared as quickly as it had appeared. Devdan ran back towards the royal garden, but when he arrived, he realized that it was already too late. He recognized his father floating in the air, but he did not look like the Elf King at all. He looked as if he was in another state of mind, an evil mind.

"Father? What is happening?" asked Devdan, but there was no response. He looked around to find Amy, but could only find the dark and ugly garden instead. He knew a little about the recent disappearances of many humans who had traveled through the land before. But he had never suspected that his own father may have been behind all of it. There were many others who had mysteriously disappeared as soon as they spent a day with the King in the royal garden. The rumors claimed that each time, a wild animal attacked them and only took the human away. Even though the King always pretended to be upset about this, he never mentioned anything about the details, but now, Devdan, the Prince of Elves himself, saw what was truly happening.

"Amy?" he shouted.

But again, there was no response, only the painful shrieking of the wind.

"What has happened here? How?" wondered Devdan.

"Don't worry, my unfortunate son. All will be well soon," responded Eltor while he was floating close to the ground.

"What? What have you done? What has happened to this place? Where is Amy?" asked the Prince worriedly.

"Oh, she will be fine. Do not worry about her, and this place just needed a remodeling that I have done. Isn't it much better this way?" asked Eltor sarcastically and started laughing, hanging eerily in the air.

"What do you mean? Where is she?" asked Devdan. "And what has happened to you?"

"I thought you would find out sooner, but apparently not. I am the one and only ruler!" announced Eltor, and then he turned into a dark monster, with his face and body all covered up in the dark shadows.

"Y-you are the 'dark figure' feared through the land?! No, no. Impossible. I must be dreaming," muttered Devdan.

"So you think that I, the mighty ruler of all, am not capable of being and doing whatever I shall please? And for you, my dear son, I see you as an obstacle in my path, so I must do what I had always planned to: Kill you!" and with that he raised his right arm and threw searing lightning bolts at him. Scared, Devdan quickly ran behind the statue in the center of the garden, and the bolts exploded the head of the statue of the King. This made Eltor even angrier than before, and he raised both his hands and threw piercing ice at Devdan's direction, but Devdan who always carried a magical, folding shield with him was able to survive the attacks.

As soon as the King was about to launch another attack at him, Devdan heard a familiar, faint voice he recognized. As he looked around, he saw Amy lying down on the ground next to the statue. Devdan quickly went to her and shook her, he even called her name, but there was no response.

"What did you want from her?" asked the Prince angrily.

"Not much, just her life force. Honestly, the only thing she had that was precious to me was her patience. I have gotten every other necessary characteristics and personality traits from the other kind people before her, and I only needed her patience to reach the full power of the King of the universe!" declared Eltor.

"So, you just killed her?" asked Devdan. "For your own selfish purposes? But how could you? She trusted you. I trusted you. I am sorry, father, but I am embarrassed to even mention your name as my father!" and he hugged Amy to his chest and started to leave.

"And where do you think you are going?" asked Eltor evilly. He raised his hands, looked up the dark sky, gathered all of his dark powers, and threw them towards Devdan and Amy with all his dark energy. Yet suddenly, a huge light appeared from Amy's heart and repelled the dark forces.

Amazed and confused, the prince bent down and felt that she was still alive after all, for she was now breathing slightly and was a bit warm to the touch. So, Devdan kneeled down and kissed Amy's forehead gently. It had been said that a kiss by an elf was able to perform magic, and he believed that it would be valuable to put this idea to the test!

Amy slowly opened her eyes and gasped for breath. At this sight, Eltor felt outraged! He suddenly fell down to the ground and started begging for help: "I feel very weak. Please help me," gasped Eltor.

"I know as well as you do that you are not weak. This must be another one of your trickeries," said Devdan.

"No. Really!" begged Eltor. "Come, Amy, my son, please help me rise."

"No. I am sorry, but I cannot," said Amy.

"Ah!" shouted Eltor and he rose up again. This time, facing Amy, he shouted with fury, "I took away your life force, so how could you still be alive?"

"The soul of a person is something that cannot be taken away. It is always within the person who possesses it . . . ," declared Amy.

"No!" shouted Eltor angrily, and with this, he summoned all his great dark powers together once again, from an infinite number of wild creatures never seen before by Amy, such as black and green fire breathing dragons and mythical centaurs to the lightening bolts and ice pieces.

Devdan drew his sword and shouted: "Get behind me!"

But as the creatures were charging towards them, involuntarily, Amy rose up to the sky, and an immense light shone from her. As soon as it touched the darkness, it made it all turn into ashes that rose up to the sky and joined the dark clouds and vanished, as it had appeared. As for the King, who was very confused at this point, he turned towards Amy and asked weakly:

"How?"

"As I told you before: A soul can never be taken away from one. Never," responded Amy strictly.

And at this, the once King of Elves slowly faded into the darkness he had created and joined the other evil forces.

# CHAPTER 10

# Home

$S$lowly, the garden transformed back into its original beauty, colorful flowers and leaves and a wonderful blue sky were returned to the once dark and evil land.

"Well, I guess this is a goodbye then," said Devdan sadly.

"I believe so. Thank you for saving my life, though," said Amy, smiling at Devdan.

"And thank you for saving mine!" said Devdan. "Here, this will help you find your way home," and he gave Amy a small mirror with a golden frame and a green jewel on the top that had the marking of a crown on it. "This is very special and it will allow you to find your way whenever you are lost. Please keep this as a memory from here and from me, and you can always come back if you ask from it,"

"Thank you very much, Devdan. Please say goodbye for me to Mylaela too," said Amy sadly.

"Sure! I really wanted to show you around here, but I think it is best that you leave now. I hope I will see you again in the future," said Devdan.

"Thank you," said Amy, wiping her tears.

She took a deep breath and looked into the mirror and said: "Please lead me back home," and she disappeared from sight.

Amy slowly opened her eyes, but could only see the blue sky and the cherry tree standing tall next to her. Quickly, she stood up and started searching for her Reverse machine, but she could not find any traces of it anywhere: *Well, maybe I had lost it at some point*, she wondered. Amy then reached into her pocket, and felt that her necklace and the mirror were still there!

*Magic*, thought Amy, and she hurried toward the house to see her grandpa again.

"Grandpa?" shouted Amy.

Grandpa was standing at the doorstep, with somewhat teary eyes.

"Back already, Amy?" asked Grandpa.

"Yes. And I am sorry I left suddenly. I love you," whispered Amy.

"I love you too. And I am sorry for everything, so shall we get ready? Your tutor should be coming soon!" said Grandpa anxiously.

"What do you mean? I should have been gone for ages!" said Amy confusingly.

"It was like ages to me as well, Amy, but in reality you have been gone for only two minutes!" admitted Grandpa.

"Really?" asked Amy, and they went back into the house.

At this moment, a knock was heard at the door.

"Would you open the door please, Amy?" asked Grandpa kindly.

"Sure!" responded Amy.

As soon as she opened the door, she saw a young man with semi-pointy ears and green, sparkly eyes, who bowed low and introduced himself: "Hello. I am Jeremy. Your Grandpa had asked me to meet with you," said Jeremy, smiling.

"B-but you are Prince Devdan . . . ? Never mind, please come in!" said Amy, and Jeremy followed her into the house.

"Oh, how very nice to see you again, Jeremy! How is your father doing?" asked Grandpa.

"Unfortunately, it has been a while since he had passed away, sir, but I have been living with my uncle now," said Jeremy.

"Oh, no! I am deeply disappointed to hear this," said Grandpa.

"It's okay. I have been growing used to it. Now, where should we begin?" asked Jeremy.

"Follow me!" replied Amy and they both went to Amy's room.

"Let me know if you needed anything," said Grandpa.

And Amy and Jeremy began reviewing their books together.